This igloo book belongs to:

Elisa ♥

igloobooks

Written by Stephanie Moss
Illustrated by Ela Jarzabek

Designed by Katie Messenger
Edited by Natalia Boileau

Copyright © 2018 Igloo Books Ltd

An imprint of Igloo Books Group,
part of Bonnier Books UK
bonnierbooks.co.uk

Published in 2019
by Igloo Books Ltd, Cottage Farm
Sywell, NN6 0BJ
Manufactured in China. GOL002 0519
10 9 8 7 6 5 4 3 2 1

Library of Congress Cataloging-in-Publication
Data is available upon request.

ISBN 978-1-83852-544-6
IglooBooks.com
bonnierbooks.co.uk

The Greatest Mommy of All

igloobooks

You're the **greatest** mommy. I love you more with every day.
There are lots of reasons why, almost too many to say.

You're always there to lean on, with a **loving** hand to hold.

If there was a Mommy Medal, I know yours would be **gold**.

No matter where we are, you always make it feel like home.
I love you because I know I'll never be alone.

I'm sure no one has as much fun as us when we're together.

You know just how to make me **laugh**, no matter what the weather.

You're the **kindest** mommy, and do you know how it shows?

You're never, ever angry, even when I tickle your **wiggly** toes!

When I'm feeling nervous, a bit lonely, or just shy . . .

. . . you're right there behind me, saying,

"It's okay to try."

You're not just my mommy, you're my **best** friend, as well.

You know all my **special** secrets. There's no one else I'd tell.

No one in the world makes a bad day **better** quite like you.

One **kiss** and a cuddle makes everything as good as new.

You could be almost **perfect**. At least that's how it seems.
You deserve a Best Mommy Award, one that glitters and gleams.

Best Mommy Award

When you sing me a lullaby, I know everything's alright.
You're the one I **dream** of when I fall asleep at night.